Bully Dogs

Jacquie Ream

BOOK PUBLISHERS NETWORK

Book Publishers Network
P.O. Box 2256
Bothell • WA • 98041
Ph • 425-483-3040
www.bookpublishersnetwork.com

10 9 8 7 6 5 4 3 2 1

Printed in the United States of America

LCCN 2009904433
ISBN10 1-935359-14-2
ISBN13 978-1-935359-14-2

Artwork: Phyllis Emmert
Editor: Julie Scandora
Cover designer: Laura Zugzda
Typographer: Stephanie Martindale

Dedicated to my friend Debbie, who, during my darkest hour, lit a candle.

Contents

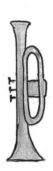

Chapter 1

Dog Days for Frances Reed

My mom's wrong. These are not my best years, and I seriously doubt I'll look back upon my childhood as the happiest days of my life.

One way or the other, I wished I'd be dead by Friday, the morning of the girls' sixth-grade volleyball team selection (that is, the Longest Hour in the Life of Frances Reed), or I knew I'd be suffering horribly after getting attacked by the bully dogs.

Maybe it would be better just to let the bully dogs eat me alive tomorrow morning. I'm getting plenty tired of running from the black Labrador, cocker spaniel, and golden retriever. Really, should I have to deal with three, big, dumb dogs that have taken a dislike to me, for what reason I have no idea? Old crotchety Mr. Wessenfeld used to walk them himself, but now he just lets them run loose.

🐾   🐾   🐾

I can't help but wonder why things are the way they are, especially about adults and what they say or do or don't bother to do at all. What gets me the most is all the preaching adults do about responsibility, and yet, no one has done anything about Mr. Wessenfeld, who lives four houses down across the street, letting his vicious mutts out every morning to do their number.

And boy, did they do a number on me! Snarling and yapping, they'd chase me down the end of the street, across Main Avenue, all the way to Saint Mary's schoolyard. Some days, I just about didn't make it to the chain-link gate that would separate me from them. And then didn't I look just great, huffing and puffing, red-faced, and sweat running down my cheeks for the start of classes? I don't have a lot in the looks department, not like some of the other girls in my class, and it really helped when I knew my scraggly brown bangs were plastered against my forehead. I'm sure I looked like a drowned mouse.

Annie, one of my best friends since second grade, told me I'm not ugly at all and understood how I felt, but I make her promise not to tell anyone, particularly Marcy, Sue, and Ursala. They would have had a field day if they'd known I'd run away from the bully dogs.

Not that "The Three Amigos" didn't already give me a bad enough time and always had since kindergarten. Especially Marcy. We'd always been together in a small class. The biggest I remember was the combined fourth and fifth grades with twenty-one students, eleven boys and ten girls. Marcy and I were a bad combo, like a hyper cat and a snarling dog stuck together in the vet's waiting room. We just didn't mix well with each other, and the less she knew about me, the less she could telegraph all over Saint Mary's barnyard with her mega-mouth. She was real quick with the nasty names that stuck, like calling me "Franny Fanny." Most people, except my mom, call me Fran.

"Frances!"

"Yeah, Mom?" A quick glance at the clock and I knew that it was time to practice the piano and then the trumpet.

"Time to practice!"

"Just another five minutes, okay?"

"No!" Suddenly she was looming in my doorway. "That's what you said at four-thirty after being on the phone twenty minutes giggling with Carol. Fifteen minutes on the trumpet, and thirty on the piano."

"But I'm doing my math!" I pointed out reasonably enough. "And I only spoke with Carol for fifteen minutes." I knew, because her mom has a timer by the phone. Carol is my very best friend, but she lives on the other end of town and goes to Saint Thomas, so we have to talk everyday so we know what's happening with each other. She's the only one that I don't mind calling or talking to on the telephone. "I'm almost done, then I'll go downstairs and practice. Okay?"

"No, now. You'll have time to finish your homework before dinner. Go." She dramatically threw her arm out, jabbing in the general direction of the stairs.

"All right, all right!" I put down my pencil and got up.

"Look," her voice erupted like a volcano, "why don't you just quit band and piano altogether? I hate these constant hassles with you."

Actually, I like playing the trumpet and don't really mind piano, though I'd been at it for five l-o-n-g years, practically half my life. Going over and over the same stuff bores me.

"So who's hassling? I'm going right now."

Her face was all pinched like she was mad. I didn't know what made her so touchy, but I wished she'd relax. As she stood there glaring at me, I picked up the pencil that had bounced off the desk and rolled onto the floor and slid it in between pages of chapter six of *The Sword in the Stone* I'd been reading.

I always practiced the trumpet first, which I liked better, I suppose, because I was good for a first-year student. Miss Kray, our school bandmaster, said that if I kept improving as I had, I'd be first chair that year.

I was careful not to spend a lot of time cleaning my trumpet, or Mom would go nuts on me, reminding me it didn't count for practice time. But I had to maintain my instrument, and I did what I had to do, then warmed up before "reviewing and renewing" band pieces for the week. After that I started the scales and triads on the piano.

Sometimes my dad would come downstairs to read the newspaper, and it'd make the time go faster. He thought he was giving me silent encouragement, but I knew he was only making sure I did my assignments. He'd always ask about my lessons, and I'd tell him Mrs. Nieman had given me another march or sonata that week.

"Good," he'd say, "let me hear you play it like Sam Spade," then laugh as he'd punch the front page in half and read on.

Sometimes I wish my older brother and sister were still at home, but most times I like being by myself with Mom and Dad. Mostly Dad. Mom and I get on each other's nerves when we spend too much time together.

"Are you going to check my math tonight, Dad?" I asked as he settled into his chair.

He snapped the paper open and replied, "After dinner, okay?"

"Mom wouldn't let me finish my math, and I've only got a couple of more problems to do. She made me come down here."

"Play it again, Fran." He waved his hand at me and buried his head into the financial section, but I saw him smiling when I started "When the Saints Come Marching In."

"Can I read the comics before dinner?" I shouted above the crescendo finish.

"When you're done!" he ended up roaring after the music had faded.

"All right, Dad, all right."

By the time he was through with the paper, I was all done with practice and got a good start on the comics.

"What about your homework?" bellowed my mom from the top of the stairs.

"In a minute; almost done." I had half a page to go, but it was no good telling her that it'd take me only another two minutes, max.

"Now, Frances." With her hands on her hips and a mean scowl, she looked just like Henry the VIII, the old head-chopper.

"Just do it," my father sighed, and I got up, finished with the last strip. My dad rattled the newspapers real loud as he collected the comics, loud enough so that I'd know he was the one picking them up, not me.

"Where's the mail?" I heard Dad ask Mom.

"Frances brought it in for me," Mom replied, then had to add, "If she put it down somewhere in her room, it'll be lost in the black hole."

I looked around my room. I knew where everything was. My shoes were beneath my uniform skirt and shirt, my science book was under my lunch sack in the corner where my stuffed animals kept watch over the defeated Redcoats, all lying dead from the last battle with the United States Army. Everything in its place, and a place for everything. Honestly, I can't figure out why Mom kept on and on about what a mess the place was. Did it really matter? After all, I could find whatever I needed.

Dad walked in, making a big show of stepping over some books I had to return to the library, and frowned. "Franny, couldn't you just throw out some of these papers?"

"Dad! Not that one. That's my English, and it's due tomorrow." I snatched it away from him and handed him three letters and the junk mail with flyers that left a trail on my desk, across my bed, and on the floor. "I'll pick those up later."

But he'd already swooped down to gather them up. "No, it's the least I can do for the cause," he said then tweaked my nose before he left.

"Dinner! Wash up!" Mom's voice echoed throughout the house. Just another three minutes and I'd be done with the last of the forty-two multiplication problems.

"Frances, please!"

I finished the last sentence of the seventh chapter of *The Sword in the Stone*, dropped a book marker in it, and quickly did the last set. "Just one more minute," I said. "One more and I'm done."

As I sat down to the dinner table, Mom looked at me and said, "You didn't wash up."

"Oops, sorry. I didn't have time." I smiled at her, but she didn't smile back.

"So how did school go today?" Dad asked as I mashed butter into the baked potato, the only good thing on my plate.

"It was okay," I replied with a shrug, just to let them know that there is nothing worth telling about the sixth grade.

"No trouble with the gruesome-twosome?" He meant Marcy and Sue, who always gave me grief. Ursala just sort of hung out with them without ever really saying or doing much.

"Nah." I looked up, and Mom was shooting daggers at me, so I took a bite of fish. "What's for dessert?"

"Spinach soufflé."

Sometimes I think my mom's serious when she's not. "Yuck!" That made her laugh, so I knew she was kidding. "That's as bad as halibut."

Wrong thing to say to her. "Eat it," she snapped.

When I grow up, I don't think Mom will ever come to my house and have dinner because I am not going to cook anything I don't like to eat and that doesn't leave much that she'll want to eat.

"Bring me your math, and I'll look it over while I'm having my strawberry shortcake." Dad winked at me.

I choked down the last bit of fish and broccoli, washed the bad taste away with milk, then ran, and got my homework. All that exercise made me hungry. "Can I have lots of strawberries and whipping cream?"

"No, Frances," of course, my mom said, "but I do have some more broccoli and fish if you want."

"No, thanks, Mom." But she brought in the beaters and bowl that she whipped the cream in and gave them to me. "All right! I'll lick 'em clean!"

"Franny." Only my dad says Franny, and I knew he wasn't pleased. "How is it you get the right answers on the hard ones and miss the easy problems?"

That's how I am, I guess. "How many, Dad?" I hoped I could call it a day and get back to my book.

"Seven silly mistakes, my girl." He handed me a pencil, eraser, and the paper. "I'll recheck them after you're done."

I worked while Mom cleared the table and started the dishes. She was almost done loading the dishwasher when Dad went over the last set.

"Could you try being a littler neater, Fran?" he asked me for the umpteenth time.

"I thought it looked pretty good." And I looked again at the seven rows of six problems.

"You might erase instead of crossing out," is all he said as he gave me back my paper.

"Sure, Dad." I kissed him on the cheek and headed for my room.

"Frances!" Mothers have fantastic timing. I put down my book and waited. "Take out the garbage."

"Right." My mother the chore-master. I slid the empty wastebasket next to her as she swept the floor. I was almost out of there when she nabbed me again.

"Honey," she leaned on the broom, "please put a liner in it for me."

"Then can I read for a while?" I inquired sweetly.

"No, dear, it's bath time." She waited with exaggerated patience for me to punch down the plastic bag into the garbage can. "And please, no books in the bath tub."

"Ah, Mom!" But I could see she wasn't going to give an inch. Shower people do not understand the necessity of relaxing in the tub with a good book after a long day. I am not going to have even one shower in my house when I grow up.

"And wash your hair."

"Anything else?"

"Brush and floss your teeth," she said with a smile the Devil would have appreciated.

Well, she sure made short work of my favorite pastime. If I was lucky, she'd be doing the crossword puzzle and forget to watch the clock, and I'd get another chapter in before lights out.

I heard her footsteps coming down the hall, nine-o-five. Just this last half of a page and…

"Mark it, Frances." Mom stood beside my bed, waiting.

But I was done before she plucked the book away from me and laid it on my desk. "Good night," she said, shaking her head and rolling her eyes up in a look of mock despair as she brushed the drippy hair from my eyes. "Sweet dreams and don't let the bedbugs bite."

I gave her a kiss for a kiss, a hug for a hug. "Love you," she whispered as she turned out the lights. "Aren't you glad tomorrow's Friday?" She closed the door, probably smiling to herself.

My heart sank.

Friday.

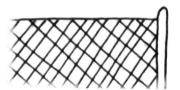

Chapter 2

Countdown

The good thing I can say about Friday was that the bully dogs stayed home. I made it to school at my usual time, just at first bell, when I could blend with the herd as we all walked through the halls to our rooms and sat at our desks. Like I said, the less I had to do with Marcy and Sue, the better my day went.

Usually.

Today was the exception, as I knew it would be. The Big Day of Sixth Grade Volleyball Team Selection. During P.E. the teams got picked. The girls' team leaders were, you might have guessed, Marcy and Sue. In front of the sixty-eight people, there seemed a 100-percent chance I would be the last and least-wanted player to be chosen.

I wasn't disappointed. Annie was picked second by Sue, and I kept hoping against hope that Sue's team would be one short at the end and have to take me.

That's the way it worked, but Sue stalled so long in doing the obvious that Mrs. Aster, the principal, finally waved me over.

"Well, now," she clapped her hands, like she always does, "that's settled, and we can draw for the serve."

Everyone knew you don't draw for the serve, but we pretty much tolerated ditzy Mrs. Aster, if only because she's the principal. So we waited, without a sigh or snicker, until our P.E. teacher, Miss Ford, finally spoke.

"Perhaps we should flip a coin for first serve." We all smiled at Miss Ford and nodded.

"Oh!" Mrs. Aster smacked her hands together again. "Then, team captains come forward!" Marcy and Sue were already standing in front of her, but they each took another step closer. "Call it, girls!"

The quarter pinged onto the floor and rolled, almost getting to the bleachers before Miss Ford stepped on it. "Heads. Marcy's serve. Line up!"

I was third to serve and got two balls over the net, but only one point. I may not be liked by the team captains, but I know I'm a good player. We're all pretty good, but Marcy and Sue are terrific at this game, fast and right there under the ball all the time, it seems.

Maybe a lot has to do with the fact they both belong to the YWCA and play on other teams after school. Ursala and Annie serve well and can return net balls. The rest of us are okay by comparison, usually botching the fab-four's serves one way or the other. But occasionally someone else saves the game with a lucky move. The teams were pretty evenly matched, and our tournament ended in a draw.

"Nice game!" Marcy slapped Sue's extended hands.

"Yeah," Sue replied, "wish we could play a real game, like against St. John's."

We all agreed. We were the only school that didn't have a girls' volleyball team in the Catholic Youth Organization. To get into the CYO league, we needed a coach, uniforms, and permission from the principal.

"Why don't we ask Miss Ford to coach us?" I suggested.

"Yeah, why don't you do that, Fran?" Marcy quipped with a toss of her long, blonde hair.

So I went over and asked Miss Ford. "Well," she hedged and then smiled, "why not? I'm sure Mrs. Aster will give us permission. You'll need money for uniforms, though. And each girl will have to pay a league fee. I'll get the necessary paperwork turned into the CYO and set up the practices at Sandalwood Junior High if you can get money for the uniforms and league fees."

Two down and one to go. Annie came up with a brilliant idea. "Let's have a car wash! The eighth grade earned enough money to go to camp, and they only had one car wash on a Saturday!"

"My dad might let us use three of his extra-long, heavy-duty hoses!" volunteered Tina, and then someone else added, "I'll bring rags and soap."

"But where are we going to have this car wash?" asked Sue. She's not only smart, but practical. "Ritchie's dad let them use his car lot on Main Street."

"That's why they got so many cars, too," grumped Ursala. "They were right on the busiest street in the city."

Marcy turned to me with a sneer. "Well, Fran, where are we going to have it? Maybe you can just go up to Ritchie and ask him if his dad will let us use his lot, too."

"I don't even know Ritchie," I shot back, trying hard not to let that too-familiar hot flush transform to tears. "But we can think of something!"

"Sure we can," Marcy rolled her eyes and then tapped Sue on the shoulder. "Let's go."

Annie and I walked back to class together. "Gee, Fran, it seemed like a good idea. Too bad, huh?"

I didn't reply, though I wished I had. It still seemed like a good idea.

Mrs. Hammershaw handed out a printed list of words as we filed through the classroom door.

"Study this list," she announced, "for the spelling bee next week."

I looked down the rows of words. Nothing I couldn't handle. Maybe I could beat Steve this year, although he had taken the regionals last year. But I had been making my own lists from the books I'd been reading, and I planned on giving it my best shot this year. Even if I wasn't a straight-A student like Steve, Marcy, Sue, Annie, and Ursala, I did better on the weekly spelling tests than anyone in class.

The dismissal bell caught us in the middle of the Spelling Round Game, just before I would have had to tackle "conceive." I guess you could say I was saved by the bell.

When I got home, my grandmother was having coffee with my mom. "How's Granny's Franny?" She grabbed me as she always did in a bear hug and squeezed me for all she was worth.

"Oh, all right, I guess." I wiggled out of her arms, which was easy because she's shorter than I am. Mom gave me the look that said "Be nice to your grandmother." As far as grandparents go, Granny's okay; she spoils me, but sometimes she treats me like I'm still six years old.

"You don't look too happy. What's wrong?" Granny slipped two pieces of caramel candies into my hand.

After unwrapping them, I popped both in my mouth and shrugged. Mom started to say something, but I remembered to add, "Thanks, Granny," only I had a big wad of candy in my mouth, and my teeth sort of stuck together, and the words came out muffled.

"Frances," my mom objected, but Granny cut in, putting her hand back around me.

"That's all right. Finish chewing it, and tell your granny what's wrong."

I'm taller than Granny, and when she drapes her arm around my shoulder, she reminds me of a puppet dancing on tiptoes.

I finally swallowed the huge caramel lump in one gulp. "You know, we could make the deadline for CYO if we could just find a place to hold the car wash, but Marcy said why don't I ask Ritchie, and I don't even know him!"

"What?!" both Mom and Granny said at the same time.

I explained the whole thing, sitting between them on the couch. I couldn't help the tears that came, even though I tried not to cry after I had said the part about not having a place to wash cars like Ritchie's dad's lot.

Granny searched in her purse for a tissue, then dabbed my face. I took the tissue from her and blew my nose. She tapped my knee. "Say, I've got an idea!"

And when Granny gets an idea, it's usually a beaut! "Why don't you ask Uncle Ryan if he'd let you have your car wash at his gas station?"

"Perfect!" I whooped, jumping to my feet. "Do you really think he'd let us?"

"Call him and find out," replied Mom. "I'll look up his phone number."

"Couldn't you call him for me?" I hated the telephone, except for special calls to my best friends, Carol and Annie. Worse than answering the loudmouthed thing when it interrupted the middle of a television program, was calling someone and going through the whole rigmarole of "Hi, how are you? I'm fine" and then trying to come up with something to say without sounding lame. But Mom, being a mother, shook her head.

"It's your project, dear. Just be done with it." She gave me a slip of paper with Uncle Ryan's number on it. "Remember to say who you are when he answers the phone."

I had to do it right then because both of them were going to sit there staring at me until I did. Luckily, Uncle Ryan answered the phone himself.

"Um." I was at my best on the opening line. "Uncle Ryan." I speeded up, and the words kind of tumbled out, "This is Fran, your sister's daughter." He sounds like he's laughing whenever I talk to him, but he's nice enough. "Granny said to call you and ask if I, I mean, my class, well, it's our volleyball team, really, can have a car wash."

"You need a clean car to play a game with volley-balls?" he joked.

"Oh, yeah, we do. I mean, we need to raise money for our uniforms, and I thought maybe you would let us use the gas station to have a car wash. We'd bring hoses, soap, rags, and buckets. There'd be about six or eight of us there."

"Do I get a percentage of the profits?" he asked all serious.

I hadn't planned on anything this complicated. "Uh, I don't know."

He burst out laughing. "I was kidding you, Fran. Sure. You want to do it on Saturday or Sunday?"

"You mean it?" I squealed, hating the way I do that when I get an answer I don't expect. "Oh, I don't know. I'll have to ask the others what day."

"Well, call me when you find out. Either day. We'll make arrangements, okay?"

"Yeah, okay!" Then I hung up, only to see that same old look of my mom's that reminded me too late that I hadn't said thank you.

"I have to call him back; then I'll thank him, okay?"

Mom didn't say anything because Granny piped up. "You'd better call your teammates and get the ball rolling," then laughed at her own joke. I laughed, too, but stopped when I thought about all those phone calls I had to make.

"Um, Granny," I began, but Mom headed me off before I could finish my sentence.

"Wouldn't it seem silly, Frances, if anyone but you called your teammates?"

"Yeah, I know."

I saw Mom taking out the list of addresses and telephone numbers from the directory. She handed me the blue sheets. "Go to it."

"Couldn't I read for just an hour? It's been a rough day, Mom." But nothing doing, not until I had done what she wanted me to do.

Because I figured it would save me a hassle, I made the decision that Saturday, noon, would be a good time for the car wash. I called Annie first, and she got all excited about our big project. She told me not to worry about telling Marcy and Sue; she would take care of it. Boy, that was a relief!

By some miracle, everyone else was home, and I got eleven girls to promise they would be there. After making three return calls and getting only busy signals, I finally got Uncle Ryan. Then I had to wait one horrible minute while I thought he'd say no, but he must have had to check his calendar or something.

"All set, Fran. You've got the time and place. Now, hope for the sun and cars."

I hung up and looked out the window. The sky was clouding up, and the wind was blowing.

"No one will want to come to the car wash if it's raining!" I felt like howling, stamping my feet, and beating up the weatherman. "I hate Seattle!"

"Oh, Frances, calm down; it's not the end of the world."

"It might as well be! The car wash is my idea." Those darn old tears came again, and my mom gave me that look that meant, "Must you cry?" but I couldn't help it. "Just once, can't things turn out right?" On top of it, I had the hiccups.

"Look, Franny, at the way the wind's blowing those old clouds. Maybe it'll just blow them away." Granny was trying her best to cheer me up.

"It could rain tonight and clear up for tomorrow," added my mom.

Granny pulled me down onto the couch next to her and began to rub my back. "Now, don't cry. Granny just knows it'll be a good day for you." When Granny says it that way, I always have hope.

"Sure."

"You know what they say, don't you, Franny?" Granny paused, shook her finger, and took a big breath to answer with "Granny's words of wisdom."

Before she could say it, Mom and I sang out in unison, "Tomorrow's always another day."

Chapter 3

Win, Lose, or Draw

*I*t rained most of the morning, until around one o'clock. Although the sky was overcast, there was no wind, and it wasn't too cold for the ten of us that showed up. Uncle Ryan let us wash his car first, and then came over with his wallet open.

"How much?" he asked.

I hadn't thought of the price, yet. "Two dollars?"

He looked over his car where Tina was still wiping off the headlights. "Fair enough. Do you guys... er...girls have a sign made up?"

I hadn't thought of that, either. "No," I said, looking helplessly at Annie. Marcy groaned. I turned around and blasted her. "Well, you didn't think of it, either!"

Before a real honest-to-goodness fight got under way, Uncle Ryan spoke up. "Look, I've got some white cardboard boxes you could break down and black felt markers to write with—just make your sign bold and clever. One or two of you should stand on the sidewalk and wave customers in."

Marcy and Sue volunteered, which suited the rest of us just fine. They certainly had the mouths for it. To be honest, they also had the spunk to wave and shout and kid around with people.

We worked like dogs all day until six that night, but made only fifty dollars. We needed at least seventy. We were all standing around, down in the dumps, when my mom drove up.

"Can I get my car washed?" She looked all happy and excited. "Nice weather for a car wash, huh?"

I threw down my rag and started collecting our stuff. "Yeah, only not enough people wanted their cars washed today. We didn't make enough money." The others were getting ready to go, too.

Uncle Ryan walked over, tossing my mom a package with windshield wipers in it. "Not a bad turnout, don't you think?"

"They didn't make their quota," my mom said softly, tapping the box against the dashboard.

"Well," Uncle Ryan turned around and, with a sweeping motion of his arm, addressed us, "why don't you do it again tomorrow? The weatherman says it's going to be a sunny day. I don't mind if you guys... er...girls come back."

Half of us were willing; half not. So six of us agreed to come Sunday at noon and hustle ten cars to wash.

Things went a lot smoother without Marcy and Sue. Ursala took the duty of walking the sign up and down the sidewalk, like an old-time town crier proclaiming a big event. We had twelve cars in four hours, mostly parents that hadn't come yesterday.

"We did it!" I shouted as I handed my mom the seventy-four dollars. "With four dollars to spare."

The six of us gave each other the high-five victory hand-slap and cheered, "Four, six, eight. Aren't WE great!" It even felt like we were a team.

"What are you going to do with the extra four dollars?" my mom asked in her most motherly, practical voice.

"Buy an extra-large pizza at the end of the season party!" chimed Rachel, which we all agreed to with enthusiasm.

"Umm," my mom stalled in her 'let's be reasonable' way, "maybe add it to the money collected at the end of the season for the coach's present?"

It was hard to argue with her logic, so I said, "Okay, keep it and buy Miss Ford something really neat."

So everything started off pretty good. Practices were set up for Tuesday and Thursday evenings, but only ten girls made it for the team. That left us with four substitutes per game, if every girl showed.

Miss Ford made us run two laps around the court before we even got started, then had us volley the ball to one another to get down the correct way to return the ball over the net. We had a practice session with the parents one night, and boy, did they have some bad habits! My mom was the worst of the lot, too, stepping out of the server's box every time. Miss Ford said she'd have to take one whole practice time to correct our return serves. Probably the next time we played our parents, if Miss Ford lets us, we would wax them if they played by the rules.

The week went by fast, and things were looking good, for a change. The bully dogs were out only one morning, and I was far enough down the street that they missed seeing me, so I made it to school without being hassled. Once at school, though, it was a different matter.

As I said, the playground is like a barnyard, and the sixth-grade boys were just like pigs. They grabbed the soccer balls before any of us girls could get to them, and the only game they let us in on was kickball, always their rules, of course, which meant they won all the time. Usually I didn't play because the rules changed in mid-game, especially if it looked as if the girls were going to score.

Marcy, Sue, Ursala, Tina, Rachel, and Annie liked to get out there and run up and down, squealing as if they were having all the fun in the world losing at the boys' game. Most times I stood by the gate and watched, not saying much, if anything.

"Hey, Marcy, why don't ya get Franny to play on your team? She could stand in front of the goal and block the ball with her big head!" Brian yelled loud enough so everyone for miles could hear.

He should talk; he was so overweight. I sneered at him in disgust, thinking that he looked just like a big hog out there, rooting in the field. "Brian, you're a porker," I muttered, not caring that he couldn't hear me.

The new kid in seventh grade, Dean, came over. He was nice but stuttered a bit, and the guys gave him a bad time about it. "Hey, Fr…Fran, want... to shoot some baskets?"

"Sure, but just a couple, okay, Dean?" I liked Dean's quiet way of asking me, and he didn't go on and on, boring me with a lot of talk about himself or stuff I could've cared less about.

As I walked over to the basketball court with him, Brian the Porker snorted, then bellowed, "Hey, lookit! Fanny and D-D-Dean! A match made in heaven!"

I got the ball on the rebound but missed the basket. Dean's face was all flushed, but neither one of us said anything. I didn't know what Dean was thinking, but I wished I'd had a good comeback. Instead, I just kept trying to get the darn ball in the basket.

"Want to practice again tomorrow, Fran?" Dean bounced the ball from hand to hand.

"I don't know. Maybe."

I glanced back at the playfield and caught the last play, just as the bell rang to go in. Steve's kick went wild, shooting out the gate, right towards the parking lot. "Stop it, Franny!" he ordered, running towards me.

Maybe he could just stop it with his mouth; I wasn't going to move a muscle. He pushed me, hard, and I fell down, my pants all muddy along the side.

Back in class, Mrs. Hammershaw asked me why I was crying. "I'm not, something's in my eye," I mumbled.

"Steve pushed Fran down on the playground, Mrs. Hammershaw." Tina pointed to Steve who looked madder than ever.

"It's all right, really," I said, trying to get to my seat without another big scene.

"No, it is not!" exclaimed Mrs. Hammershaw. "Steve, I wish to have a conference with you."

The room got real quiet, except you could almost hear everyone's thoughts about Steve, who never got into trouble, the one-and-only hotshot in soccer, basketball, and baseball and an A student, and my putting him on the bad side of the teacher. I wished it had been the bully dogs after me, instead.

Steve had to write me a note of apology, only he made sure to add a part about it being my fault that he had to shove me out of his way to get to the ball that I wouldn't stop. I jammed the note inside my trapper-keeper with all the other papers and left it at that.

And wouldn't you know it? Steve and I tied the last round of the spelling bee. I had to hand it to him, though, he got some pretty tough words—"synonym" and "self-explanatory"—but I got lucky and spelled "pseudonym" correctly. Our rematch would be the spelling bee with the seventh-graders tomorrow.

In the bathroom during the last morning recess, I overheard Sue talking to Rachel. "I hope she doesn't make it. Steve deserves to win more than she does."

I didn't linger washing my hands long enough to hear what Rachel replied, but I could guess it wouldn't have made me feel any better. I didn't want to tell them, but they were wrong. I don't think that you deserve to win because you're liked but because you've done the best. And if you lose, no big deal; you can try again.

I did feel a lot better after acing a math test, but it seemed the day had been too long. I checked what I had written down on my homework-to-do pad and realized I'd left out some of the assignments that were up on the board. That meant I still had to do religion and science, as well as English. My day was shot, what with piano lesson and volleyball practice that night. If I stayed in for last recess, I could finish my English and I'd have at least a little reading time before lights-out.

Which worked out fine because I had the feeling I wasn't welcomed out at the barnyard, anyway. I also wasn't much inclined to talk to the playground supervisor, our principal, Mrs. Aster. Her favorite subject was religious principles and how they applied to each individual's life. She used a lot of words, but it seemed she didn't make a lot of sense.

"Now, do I have your attention?" she'd always start off a lecture. "Can anyone tell me how the Golden Rule applies to our everyday lives?"

Usually someone in the seventh or eighth grade would spout something meaningful with a straight face, and you'd get the feeling that Mrs. Aster was going to reach out and pat that person on the head. Sure, every one of us could give an example, but I'm willing to bet none of us thought twice about it when Mrs. Aster left the room. And if there were a few minutes before Mrs. Hammershaw came to lead us back to our room, you can bet there was a lot of joking about what "do unto others" really meant in our daily lives. Mrs. Aster should've heard some of the things the kids said at recess when no adult was around. Boy, would she have gotten an earful of "meaningful dialogue."

The only thing I hated, no, disliked (I reserved *hate* only for certain people), more than recess was singing with Mr. Breen every Thursday at two o'clock. He was a fussy little man in a wrinkled suit, white shirt, and out-of-date tie, who waved his arms a lot and urged the girls to sing without breaking for a breath and yelled at the boys to pay attention. The songs were all too high for comfort, to sing or listen to, but we had to give an hour each week toward "music appreciation." I couldn't tell you how much I appreciated it being over at three.

I was glad my mom was waiting to take me to my piano lesson and all I had to do was walk across the parking lot to the car. One less potential run-in with the bully dogs. I liked going to Mrs. Nieman's house for my forty-five minute lesson because it counted as practice time and she was a cheerful type of person that smiled a lot. Not that she didn't come down on me like a ton of bricks when I hadn't completed all my music theory or I'd skipped an assignment! But mostly we had a pleasant enough session. If there was a minute or two to spare before my mom came, Mrs. Nieman would tell me some interesting historical facts about musicians and composers that I liked. I always had a question for her, and sometimes she gave me a book I could take home to read. Mom would give me five minutes off of practice time for reading about music, so I'd try to borrow the bigger books.

"So, how'd it go today?" my mom asked for the thirteenth time already that afternoon.

"Fine, wonderful, great, good," I replied, then looked quickly to see if I'd overdone it and annoyed her. "I aced my math test."

"How was the spelling bee?" she said, with a little note of hope in her voice.

"Oh, it's a draw. Our rematch will be in the next round with the seventh graders. Then all-school, inter-school, city, and regional."

"You seem pretty confident that you can do it." She pulled into McDonald's drive-thru and asked, "Are you thirsty?"

"Yeah! You bet!" I laughed because it was a joke between us. She says that the first thing I say when I get into the car is "I'm thirsty," but I hadn't said it that day, and that made it even funnier. I figured she'd probably say "Gotcha."

"Gotcha." Then she laughed, and I laughed even harder.

"Can I have a medium coke?" I knew she'd be surprised I wasn't asking for a large one. "And fries?" She was in a pretty good mood and maybe she'd go for the extra inch she always accuses me of taking.

"Oh, all right." She gave me that 'I'm indulging you' look. "I guess it won't hurt this time."

"Hey, since we have volleyball practice at seven, can I have dinner here?" I knew I was pushing it, but I went for the off-chance she'd say yes.

She ordered fries and a medium coke. "No," she said a bit louder than necessary, I thought, "we're having beef stew tonight."

"All right, my favorite! With those muffins, too?" I poked the straw into the lid, real careful so the drink didn't squirt out.

"Yes, ma'am." Mom smiled and pointed at a rainbow over the Nike-shoe billboard. "We should go look for the proverbial pot of gold at the rainbow's end."

"Yeah," I agreed, happy enough with the way the day was turning out, after all. Little did I expect what was going to happen at volleyball later on.

Chapter 4

"Possibilities"

Our sixth-grade girls' volleyball team had a practice match with the seventh-grade boys. I saw Dean on the sidelines, but he didn't get to play that game. He saw me, too, and waved. I said "Hi" as I walked by him to get into my position. I stayed in the whole game and managed to score eleven points in the three sets, which I thought was pretty good.

Apparently, Marcy didn't. She made it plain, loud and clear in front of everyone, that I wasn't in the right place at the right time. "Hey, Fanny, why don't you try hitting the ball over the net, not under it?" she yelled, then stomped to the server's square. She smacked the volleyball so far out of bounds she could have scored two points if we'd been playing basketball.

But no one said anything to her, at least nothing nasty. "Good shot!" cried Sue, clapping, and everyone laughed. Except me. It seemed if Ursala, Sue, Annie, or Marcy goofed up, it was all one big joke and "too bad," but if anyone else made a mistake, it was a crime against the team. Not only at volleyball, but in all the other sports, too.

Sometimes being around them made me so mad I wanted to explode, but tonight I felt deflated, like all the air in me had been let out at once, and I couldn't find the energy to speak up. We played for two games out of three, and Marcy kept up a running commentary on my mistakes the whole time.

We won one, lost two to the boys. Dean got to play, and I was secretly glad that he was better than anyone would have thought. He didn't say much to any of the guys, or to anyone for that matter, but went about his business as if he didn't care what others were doing or thinking. He managed to get the ball over the net on his serves and when it came to him. The last game, we lost by one point. Most of the seventh-grade boys stayed long enough afterwards to tell us that we were pretty good and they hoped we would win our game against St. John's. Marcy and Sue said they would stay after our game to watch the boys play and root for them. I wasn't sure I could make a promise like that without checking it out with my mom first. And I'm sure that's why the rest of the girls didn't say anything, either, to the boys before they left.

Miss Ford said we had a good chance at winning, especially if we played as a team, not as individuals. I wished she would have looked right at Marcy when she spoke to us.

"Lots of teamwork, girls. Remember, front row helps out back, and middle moves in on the other side's serve. You did an excellent job tonight—those boys have been together as a team since fourth grade, and you saw how it makes a difference. Teamwork!" She slapped her clipboard so loud that it startled all of us.

Then she laughed, waving us good-bye. "Good night, and see you Thursday at seven. On time!"

Seemed to me, she had meant every girl had done a good job, at least the best she could tonight.

Of course, not everyone would've agreed with me. Marcy, Sue, and Ursala were standing out on the sidewalk waiting for their ride. "Wouldn't it be nice if Fran found another hobby, like basket weaving?" Marcy said as I passed by.

"Just ignore her," Annie advised. "What does she know?"

I swallowed hard before I found my voice. "I wish she weren't so good at sports."

"Yeah," Annie sympathized, "but she makes mistakes, too. We all do, Fran. And aren't you always saying 'it's just a game'?"

"Yeah, but it doesn't seem like just a game when someone's yelling at you in front of everyone."

"I don't know why she thinks she can tell everyone what to do. Maybe it's because she's so good that Miss Ford lets her." Annie shrugged.

Even though I felt better talking to her, I didn't think I could explain to Annie so she'd really know how I felt. Marcy never yelled at her and made snide remarks to her as she walked by.

"See you tomorrow, Annie."

"How'd practice go, Frances?" Mom handed me a book that had come in the mail from the library.

"Uh, great." I snatched the book out of her hand as we pulled away from the curb. "We played the seventh-grade boys, but lost two out of three games."

"I think it says a lot for your team that you could win one game against a stronger team. The boys start a month earlier, and haven't they played a year longer than you girls?"

"Uh, yeah," I answered, burying my nose between the cover of *The Wind in the Willows*. For at least the rest of tonight, I'd have better things to think about than volleyball.

What I like best about reading good books is getting away from "real" life. Even though whatever happens in a story couldn't happen in my life, I know how the character feels going through the good and bad stuff. I sometimes wished I could have the opportunity to face the same challenges, and hopefully, win. And I'd like to make the good things in the stories real in my world here and let all the bad things in the world just be ideas on pages of a book. Then the heroes and heroines could take care of all the evil in the books, and we would have all the good right here in our world.

I wondered, though, was it possible to be good all the time? I'd try, but Mom would always find something wrong, at least once a day. Like that evening.

"Frances," she'd began to scold, "please pick up your towel and hang it up. And let the water out of the tub and dry your hair."

"At least I took out the garbage," I muttered, doing all the tasks she'd asked me to do.

"But you forgot to put in the liner." My mom always had to have the last remark to anything I'd say.

"But I took it out without you having to ask, didn't I? And I hung up my clothes before you said to. And put extra paper towels under the sink and swept the porch a little." She shook her head and was about to interrupt me so I headed her off, "I know; I said 'a little.'"

"I was just going to say that you're right. I'm guilty of not telling you how much I appreciate the things you do. I guess it doesn't hurt to remind me." Before I could say anything, she added, "Once in a while."

I at least got to sleep with a smile, having won that round with my mom. I only wished that I had spoken up and pointed out to Marcy the good things I'd done for the team.

Or I could have so easily avoided the bully dogs on my way to school the next morning. Like torpedoes, they came at me from the bushes I hadn't ever noticed growing in the Delong's front yard. I made a mad dash for the short cut across the corner-store parking lot and ditched all three dogs. I heard the screech of brakes but didn't turn around. If one of them got hit, please, I prayed, let it be the big, black Lab, although I immediately revised that prayer. I didn't want those creatures of my nightmares to be killed, particularly chasing me, but it did occur to me there would be an element of justice in it.

All that running made me early that morning, and Annie wasn't waiting by the doors. Marcy and Sue were there, so I stood by the railing on the top stair and took out my book to begin another chapter.

"Hello, Fran," Ursala said to me as she passed by to join Marcy and Sue.

"Hi," I replied but saw no reason to stop reading to chat. Besides, she probably wouldn't have stopped to talk with me with Marcy and Sue right there to see her.

"Good luck in the spelling bee today," Ursala said to me as we filed down the hall to the classroom.

I was too stunned to say anything but, "Thanks." It was funny, but until then I hadn't thought of anyone wishing for me to win. I just didn't know if she meant it for real or if she and Marcy would get a good laugh out of it if I didn't win.

There's Mass before first recess, and we all have to attend. Today Father Gavin reminded us that the Apostles didn't come by their faith easily and that we should look deep into our hearts and make a commitment to God. Sometimes just getting to school was commitment enough for me, let alone worrying about whether I had any faith or not; but other times, like today, I wondered if I had enough faith. I didn't think I would have wanted the life of an Apostle, that's for sure, although it would have been neat to have known Jesus Christ.

I wondered if Christ ever sweated out a spelling test when he was just a kid learning in the temple. Maybe he didn't have to learn how to spell with twelve Apostles to write it all down for him. Maybe, instead, he had to learn how to speak in front of a crowd, which would have been a thousand times harder for me to do.

Tina and I got picked to be hall monitors for the morning. We made sure everyone who left the classroom had a pass and that there wasn't a mess of books or papers left anywhere outside in the hall. If someone needed to go to the office or the nurse, one of us had to be an escort. I didn't mind being a monitor because then I didn't have to go out to recess and play in the barnyard. And sure enough, Steve got a ball kicked in his face and had a bloody nose, so I told Tina she had better walk him to the nurse's office. I sure the heck didn't want to be the one walking beside him with all that blood streaming from his nose and splattering his jacket. He would have found some excuse to get mad at me about it, I was sure.

Steve was still in the nurse's office ten minutes before the spelling bee. I got a little nervous, wondering if he was going to make it back when Mrs. Hammershaw called me over to her desk.

"Fran, would you go check on Steve and ask him if he feels well enough to be in the spelling bee?" She handed me a pass, and I hurried down the hall.

Steve was sitting up on the cot, a washcloth pressed over his nose and his head thrown back, just touching the window sill.

"Mrs. Hammershaw wants to know if you're well enough to go to the spelling bee. We have to be there in five minutes." I watched the traffic zipping by the window above his head, trying to think of all the places the people might have been going.

Steve tossed the washcloth onto the little stainless steel table and got up. "I'm all right, now. It was just a little nosebleed."

I pointed out the obvious to him. "That's an awful lot of blood all over your jacket. Why don't you take it off?"

"Why don't you mind your own business, Franny?" But he took off the jacket as we came to the auditorium and stuffed it behind a trash can by the door.

It seemed a thousand eyes followed us as we climbed the stairs upstage. Conversations rippled through the building, and you could hear bursts of laughter and groans as the lower grades came in to be seated. The room seemed hotter than it should have been and got louder as the shuffling of feet mixed with squeaky voices and deep-throated whispers.

I saw Timothy load spit balls in his mouth and aim at Annie's neck. Sue turned around and gave him a dirty look when one hit her on the ear. I almost cracked up when I saw Marcy's ponytail turning white. But it was a sure thing that Timothy was going to get caught once Marcy reached back to fluff her hair.

"Gross!" she wailed, her voice lifting over all the other noise. "Gross!!" she screamed again, as the pellets rained down like huge hunks of dandruff.

No one ratted on Timothy, though. Mrs. Aster tapped the microphone until everyone quieted. Before she could say anything, a piercing wahhhaahhhhh echoed from the mike, and it took five minutes to get the cord fixed to that the awful sound stopped.

By then, we were all trying to stifle yawns and stretch without seeming to move. We all could have died of terminal boredom before anyone would have learned how to spell it.

Mrs. Aster raised her hands and asked for God's blessing. "And children," she began with an attempt at humor, "only angels may whisper the answers to the contestants. Let's all be real quiet and listen, perhaps learn, too. Good luck to our two sixth graders and to all of our seventh graders. Let's begin."

"Fran," Mrs. Morety's clear voice demanded my attention, for sure, "you'll start us off with 'possibilities'".

I wiped my sweaty palms down the smooth corduroy of my pants and stood up, thinking if I could only find my voice, I might yet get it right.

NINTYNINE ENTRANCE HITCHHIKE OVERRATED MYTHOLOGY
NATURALLY ASTROLOGY POSSIBILITIES WINDSHIELD PERFORMANCE
WHEELCHAIR ZUCCHINI

Chapter 5

Team Spirit

"Possibilities" was a good start for me. Steve and I hung in there for the entire seventh-grade-level words. It surprised me half of the students couldn't make it beyond the first round.

Actually, we'd had most the words—overrated, wheelchair, windshield, hitchhike, and ninety-nine—in our advanced reading groups. Steve and I were in the blue group, the eighth-grade Readers, and so far none of the words had tripped up either one of us. By the third round, the eighth graders had dropped like flies sprayed with Raid.

There were four us left, and I felt pretty confident I would make it to the inner-schools contest. I almost stumbled on "succession" but added the second "s" instead of a "t" at the last minute. I noticed

Steve looking intently at me, as if he thought for sure I would miss it.

He got "zucchini" and almost ate it but stalled only long enough to spell it right. "Astrology" was too much for the last eighth-grade girl, and I felt lonely with two guys and the big words about to be pulled out for the final round.

Well, it went pretty quickly, after all. "Entrance" and "naturally" got the other two eighth graders, Steve spelled "mythology" without a hitch, and I got through "performance" without a slip. I heaved a sigh of relief and smiled back at Steve as we walked to class.

"Next week'll be us against the two best from Holy Cross and St. Michael's." Steve slowed down before we got to the door. "If you get past them, it's you against seven in the all-city. It's a written test for the regional."

"Well," I shrugged, running my finger along the wall, "I think we might, at least, get an easy A in spelling for this quarter."

"Yeah, I think you're right." Steve swung the door wide, and I had to sidestep out of the way real fast or I'd have gotten clobbered.

We were just in time for P.E. and filed right back out with our class. The boys got the soccer field, and the girls got the volleyball court. Miss Ford ran down a few tips, gave the serve to the eighth-grade girls, and then left us to a practice game while she drilled the boys in mid-field defensive maneuvers.

We took the game away from the eighth graders and were all feeling pretty good about it. Marcy, Sue, Ursala, and Annie were talking to the team captain of the eighth graders.

"You guys won by only two points!" Tracy squared off with Marcy, looking her down as she spoke. "And you've been practicing twice a week. Not our team. I'm lucky to call them together once during the week before a game."

"Boy, I know what you mean. It's hard to get everyone to show up for practice, let alone the games." Marcy puffed up with her own importance as if she'd been our captain forever. Actually, Miss Ford rotated team captain every game so each girl had the chance at being a leader, so for Marcy to have put out that she was our team captain wasn't exactly true, but she sure let on as if she were the one and only all the time.

Marcy had the exact same expression as Tracy, the weary leader look. "I just wish we had a few more good players and fewer bad ones, know what I mean? We have four wins, one loss, though. The last two games, we had only one sub, which meant some players stayed in longer and didn't do so good, know what I mean?"

Tracy looked a little irritated when she replied. "Yeah, but seems to me you have a pretty good team.

If you win this game Saturday, you're in the play-offs, so I don't see why you're making such a big fuss."

"Oh, we're pretty good," Marcy piped up, "but we could be a lot better."

Steve, Mark, and John came over to talk to us. Steve punched the ball out of Rachel's hands and bounced it down court to make a basket. I ran down to intercept the ball. It circled the rim and popped out, right into my hands. Steve made a grab for it, but I pulled the ball away, about to put it in the basket when Miss Ford blew the whistle for us to go inside. Steve popped the ball out of my hands.

"You know, Franny," he dribbled the ball up the stairs, "you're pretty good at serving the volleyball. We're playing St. John's basketball team Saturday morning, so we'll be there when you guys start your game. Their basketball team is lousy, so it's going to be a real short game."

Steve might have been the best all-around athlete, but it got to me the way he always assumed his team would be undefeated, although even I had to admit that he had to be good since his team rarely lost unless he didn't play. But still, I felt he could be wrong. "I wouldn't be so sure that you can take the game that easy. Maybe they've practiced a lot and are better now."

He twirled the ball on his finger and then pitched it to me. "I know we can take the game that easy, Fran. Trust me."

And he was right. Saturday as we lined up for pre-game drill, the boys' basketball team showed up on our side of the gym. Steve cupped his hands over his mouth and hollered, "Hey, Fran! I told you it would be easy!"

I nodded at him and caught the quizzical looks of Mom and Granny as they tried to figure out what Steve had meant. They motioned for me to come over and talk to them, but I ignored them. This was our most important game, and I wanted to do my best, without any distractions.

Everyone looked pretty good in our blue and yellow uniforms; not one jersey was even wrinkled.

Miss Ford made Stella, the smallest girl on our team, the captain, and she called "heads" but the quarter flipped on its tail side. Although St. John's got first serve, they lost it after scoring only one point.

We took the first game by three points. During the huddle before the second game, Sue whispered fiercely, "I want us to win *this* game!"

Well, didn't we all? I was team captain and mighty relieved to win the serve. Marcy scored five points the first round before losing the serve because Tina in the first row didn't return the ball over the net. You could see Marcy's face screwed up in anger, but she didn't say anything. The other team kept the ball for nine points and then lost it on a net ball. Sue picked up eight points on her serve, losing the last return when I missed the ball. I had it, until Marcy went for it, stepping in front of me, so naturally I thought she was going to get it, but she didn't.

"Stupid!" she hissed at me. "You should have had it! Get up closer to the net!"

I didn't have time to tell her that she was the one that had stepped out of her position, in my face, and muffed the play. Suddenly, the score was tied, then game point for the other team.

All along, the boys had made enough noise cheering for us to rattle the bones of a corpse, but you could hear the parents over everyone else. Except for my mom. She comes to every game, but she just sits on the sidelines and watches. Granny whoops and hollers at us, then gives me all sorts of "pointers" after the game. I listen politely but don't take anything she says too seriously. I don't think they even had volleyball way back when she went to school.

Marcy, all red in the face, stomped off the court. Miss Ford called me out for the first half of the next game, and then I got back in time to rack up the winning five points of our third game. We made playoffs, but I wasn't as happy as the rest of the team. You would have thought Marcy, Sue, and even Annie, who had played well all three games, had won without any help from the rest of us the way they carried on about this play and that play they had made. I didn't stick around to talk with anyone, not even Annie.

Granny pounded me on the back. "Let's go celebrate with a sundae. What do you say?"

"All right," I said, sliding into the back seat of my mom's car.

Mom looked in the rear view mirror at me, speaking so soft I almost missed what she said. "Frances, you're going to have to stand up to Marcy sometime, or she'll push you around forever."

"I know, Mom, I know. Please drop it. I mean, we won the most important game, didn't we?"

"And you played well!" crowed Granny. She smiled so big her teeth flashed in the bright sunshine streaming through the windshield. She turned around to face me. "You have to get under that ball and keep your eye on where it is. But my, you've improved! And I was really proud of how you kept your cool when that little snit, Marcy, yelled at you. I might have popped her one right in the old kisser, but I'm glad you had your wits about you! No, siree, you did just right by keeping calm and collected."

What she didn't realize, and I wasn't about to tell her, was that I had almost started crying on the court, and I was so shaky that, when Miss Ford called me to the benches, I was glad to sit down for five minutes.

Then I was mad enough to go back in and prove to Marcy that I wasn't stupid at all.

"Well," Mom said as she parked the car at Baskin-Robbins Ice Cream Store, "this has been some week! First you go all the way to inner-schools spelling contest, and now your team makes the league play-offs. I'd say this is at least a double-scoop-sundae-with-two-toppings sort of commemoration."

"All right by me," I said stepping up to the counter to order. "I'll have a Jack and Jill, vanilla and chocolate. With extra sprinkles."

And that was the last good thing that happened to me.

Chapter 6

Advice

Thursday morning on my way to school, I went through list after list of words that I had memorized. That's why I didn't see the bully dogs as they came around the corner on Main Avenue. I heard first a low rumble; then they were so close so fast I thought the black Lab would nab me before I got to the gate. I picked up a long, thick stick, and threw it as hard and far away as I could. Wonder of wonders! All of them all chased after it and left me alone. Seething mad, I watched them and wished a car would come along and at least scare some sense into them, but not one came down the street.

That started my day, and it got worse. I almost missed the school bus that took Steve and me over to the high school where we were competing in the inner-schools spelling contest. I didn't last the second round. I misspelled "comprehensive" with an "i" after the "h," which I knew the minute I said it was wrong. But too late; I was out of the running. Steve stayed in and won, placing in the city finals, eligible for the regionals. He met me coming out of the auditorium on the way to the bus pick-up.

"Good going, Steve." I left enough room on the bench if he wanted to sit down, too. "You really got some hard words. Like 'maneuver.' I never would have gotten that one."

I had my hand marking my place in *The Sword and the Stone*, ready to resume reading if Steve didn't feel like talking. But he did. "You got some hard ones, too, Fran. You did all right, until 'comprehensive.' That's a tough one for everyone. Except me."

"Yeah," I agreed half-heartedly. "I hope you do as well in the regionals." I meant that, hoping he would win, but I wished he could take a little less interest in himself.

"Oh, I will. I've studied pretty hard this year." The school bus lumbered up the drive, making so much racket that talking anymore was impossible. Steve got a window seat on the right side, third aisle, and I took a window seat on the left side behind the bus driver.

At the classroom door, Mrs. Hammershaw greeted us, clapping as we walked into class. I almost felt better, until I saw Marcy glaring at me as if I had done something. What now? I thought, sitting down and pulling out my math book. I saw the notice on the board from Miss Ford that practice was canceled for tonight, but there would be a make-up on Friday night, all girls to attend. Maybe Marcy was mad about that since she either went to a movie or rented a video on Friday nights. Who knew? I wondered if Annie was going to tell me anything at recess.

I had a chance to talk with Annie in the bathroom after computer class. She spoke fast, in a raspy sort of whisper.

"Oh, Fran, I'm glad you weren't here at lunch! Mrs. Perkins was on playground duty, and she grabbed Marcy by the arm and was shaking her and telling her she had no right to be mean to you Saturday at the volleyball game."

I didn't laugh, but just imagining it made me want to. "What did Marcy do all the time Mrs. Perkins had a hold of her arm?" I didn't think Marcy would have just stood there.

"Oh, she jerked her arm back and told old Mrs. Perkins that she'd be mean and say whatever she wanted to, to anyone she wanted to! She gave it right back to the old bag!"

I didn't ask Annie what she thought about the way Marcy had come down on me because I got the feeling she thought Marcy was pretty cool for having stood up to Mrs. Perkins. "I guess you could say Marcy knows how to defend herself against criticism."

I flipped water from my hands, spraying Annie like I always did.

"Fran, don't do that, okay?" She scowled at me while wiping her eye carefully.

I suddenly noticed that she was wearing mascara. I opened my mouth to ask when she had started using make-up, which was against the school rules, when she patted my arm and looked at me sympathetically.

"The only thing," she said, tugging my arm to hurry me along to class, "is that Marcy's mad at you."

So that was it! "Why me?" I protested, skidding us to a stop. "I didn't ask Mrs. Perkins to defend me, did I? I wasn't even there!"

"I know," whispered Annie before she darted through the door, leaving me with a one-sided discussion going around and around in my head.

That might have been the end of it, but of course, it wasn't. That night, when I was taking my bath, Mom got a telephone call from Mrs. Perkins. I think if Merlin had appeared in my life just then, I would've had a hard time figuring out what magical spell for him to use. Turn Mrs. Perkins into a donkey or Marcy into a toad? No, I think I would have asked him to make me disappear, for good, into another time and space, another dimension.

King Arthur I'm not, and I'm not real sure what Arthur would have done, anyway, if he'd been in my spot. What could I say to my mom that hadn't already been said and done?

"Frances, I'd like to discuss something with you. Please wash up quickly, and after you've brushed and flossed your teeth, come to the dining table."

I sometimes wonder, if the house were burning down, if my mom would insist I brush and floss my teeth before I escaped.

"Isn't it kind of late for me to be up?" I asked as I sat down across the table from her.

"We'll only be a minute. Well, Frances, when it rains, it pours, huh?" She rubbed the spot over the bridge of her nose, as if she could have smoothed out everything. "Before I get into what Mrs. Perkins had to say, I want to commend you, again, for doing your best in the spelling contest. I don't think I had your poise when I was twelve, let alone the nerve to get up like that in front of all those people and rattle off those fifty-cent words. You did a good job, kiddo."

What could she say? She's my mother, right? A good job, but not good enough. "Yeah, I tried."

"You gave it your best, and that's worth more in the long run. But onto our other topic of discussion."

She paused and sighed, I suppose, trying to put her thoughts in 'good order' as she always says. "Mrs. Perkins said she had a little run-in on the playground with Marcy. You know about that?" I responded with a nod. "She said she was taken by surprise at the way Marcy sassed her. Apparently, Marcy told her mother that Mrs. Perkins hurt her when she grabbed her arm. Mrs. Perkins maintains that she didn't grab Marcy at all." Mom sighed and looked at me with a raised eyebrow. "I'm sure Marcy's story is somewhat exaggerated."

I was sure it was, too, but I was just as sure she'd tell her mother only what she wanted her to know about what had happened. I didn't say anything, so Mom went on.

"This is a most unfortunate incident, for a couple of reasons. I agree that you shouldn't be bullied by Marcy. I saw what happened, how she stepped in front of you, and when she missed the ball, blamed you. That is inexcusable. But," Mom looked me right in the eye, and I felt guilty that I hadn't done anything to defend myself, "it happened on the volleyball court."

Significant pause, like I was supposed to know the meaning. But I didn't raise my hand and offer any answer.

"Your coach," my mom supplied her own answer, "has the responsibility of her players—not the parents in the bleachers, or the umpire." She rolled the edge of the placemat while her voice got sharper. "I refuse to fight your battles on court or off, Frances. One day you might decide that you've had enough of Marcy pushing you around. But only you can decide for yourself when and how much you'll take." She was winding her lecture up, thank goodness. "I told Mrs. Perkins I appreciated her intervening on your behalf, but it is your coach's problem, and you might want to discuss this with Miss Ford. But you might take some advice: don't talk about this at school or at volleyball. There's been too much made about this already. Okay?"

"Yeah," I mumbled and took myself off to bed. Like I said, my mom sits on the sidelines and watches, not getting involved in the games.

But she had a point. Maybe Miss Ford would take care of it and I wouldn't have to say anything, let along do anything, to draw attention to a problem I'd rather did not exist.

Which happened, in a way. Miss Ford lectured all of us on sportsmanship and team effort, not naming names. We drilled extra long on staying in our positions and using strategy for the upcoming game. One thing she warned us about that I thought we needed to hear: we couldn't get overly confident of our abilities. We were going to be up against the best teams in the league, and just because it had seemed easy up until now, it could be lost as easily as it had been won. I knew that from the spelling contests.

Marcy and Sue acted as if I was invisible the whole time of the game and afterwards. I played hard, too hard at first, and botched every serve until I stopped caring what they thought of me. Then, backwards as it seemed, my serves and returns went fine. We won the first two games, and I think all of us felt pretty tough, like we could take on the next division if we had to.

The thing I didn't like was that Annie was acting too much like Marcy, wiggling around and tossing her newly permed, long hair like a spastic horse. Ursala didn't ever seem to change, win, lose, or draw. She was kind of quiet most of the time, anyway, except at the rally part of the game, and then you could hear her voice for a mile. But it was a sweet sounding voice, and she always had a nice thing to say about the other team.

On my way out to the car, I asked Annie to call me when she got home. "It'll be later this afternoon," she promised. "I'm going to the mall with Sue, Ursala, and Marcy right now."

I guess you could say I was a bit surprised, but I merely shrugged and went on home. When she did call, all she talked about was the latest look in leather. Like we were going to wear leather pants and skirts. I didn't have much to say to her, so our conversation was short.

But I got to spend the night with Pattie, and we called Carol a couple of times with new jokes we made up. Pattie was good at thinking up the story-line, and I was good at the punch line. We had Carol laughing so hard she had the hiccups. Even her eight-year-old brother she was babysitting thought our jokes were funny.

I told Pattie about some of my problems at school. "Gee," she said as she brushed my hair into a ponytail, "I don't know why they treat you so mean. Are you mean to them?"

"No." I threw away my Juicy Fruit gum and folded two fresh sticks into my mouth. "That's just the way it's been since kindergarten."

"Well, Fran," Pattie had this big-sister voice that she used all the time on her younger brother and sister, "you're pretty and smart and good in sports, too. Don't let them make you feel you aren't. Maybe they're jealous of you."

"Right, like I have something they don't. My grandmother says I should smack Marcy right in the kisser."

"One time ought to do it." Pattie looked so serious I cracked up. "It'd sure shut her up."

"I can't hit her. I don't want to hit anyone." I was glad to have friends like Pattie and Carol, even if I didn't take their advice. I'd have to be real mad to hit Marcy, and I didn't think I could get that mad.

That's how little I knew about myself. Monday when I discovered my lunch missing from my blue backpack, I was just mad enough to hit the person who took it. Of course, no one knew who had taken it; no one saw who returned it after lunch was over. Like no one knew who had clapped an eraser all over my chair, which I didn't realize until I stood up and looked at my pants. I had to explain to my mom why my uniform was all messed up the first day of the week.

She shook her head. "Maybe someone accidentally took your lunch and was too embarrassed to return it. The chalk on your desk might have been someone's idea of a joke."

I pulled my lunch sack out of my backpack. "I don't think it was an accident, at all. And I'm not laughing, Mom."

She shook her head and sighed real hard. "You're right, honey. Who do you think did it?"

Did she really have to ask? I did a fake surprise, "Oh! Maybe it was Marcy!"

"What are you going to do about it, Frances?" Leave it to my mom to get right into the icky part of the problem.

"I don't know," I admitted after a long pause. "I guess I'll do nothing. Ignore her."

"May I offer a suggestion, Frances?"

Usually I didn't take my mom's suggestions because it meant that I'd have to do something I didn't like. But I listened patiently. "Sure, offer me a suggestion."

"I think we both agree that there is a problem with Marcy. Right?"

"Right." I chewed on a pencil, waiting for the big line.

"So, tell Marcy you thought better of her, thought she was more mature. Then offer to let bygones be bygones."

I had to laugh out loud! "Just go up to her and say, 'You've been a brat, and I don't like it! Now let's be friends.' Hah! It won't work!"

But I saw Mom was convinced her view was the right one as she pressed home her point. "I think one day you two might end up being friends, especially on the sports field. You've got everything she's got, if not more. Confidence, Frances, is what you don't have. It's the only thing you don't have that the others do."

All well and good for my mother to say, but little did she know. I certainly found out the next day from the others what else I didn't have.

Chapter 7

Invisible Girl

It turned out to be a drizzly morning, dark clouds overcast, but not cold. My sweater felt good. A jacket would have been too heavy and hot, and I would have ended up carrying it all the way, but I had a hard time convincing my mom I didn't need it. Because she's cold, she thinks I'm cold, and it just isn't so. Finally, I told her I'd carry it, not wear it, and she became reasonable and said it was up to me.

I was in no mood for the bully dogs as they came after me, so I picked up a thick, short branch and was going to swat the Lab across his nose, but Old Man Wessenfeld yelled for them, and they went scurrying home. They turned around so fast they ran into each other, like three clowns trying to get their act together. Annie wasn't on the playground or by the doors, so I read until the bell rang to go in.

It was a pretty quiet morning after prayers were said and reading groups assigned. I got promoted another level, and I dreaded having to deal with the thicker packets of worksheets. Steve and I were in the same group, and like always, he was all smiles and quips.

"Hey, Franny, this is no problem; this is easy."

Easy for him, but I had to work at it. I don't know how it was for the other two in our group, but I almost wished that I wasn't so good in reading, because it wasn't only spelling "comprehensive" that I had trouble with; it was reading comprehension. The questions get harder and the answers more confusing each level, but I supposed I'd manage to get through those last eight weeks of school all right.

If only I could have gotten through school without having to deal with Marcy, Sue, Ursala, and my one-time friend, Annie. I found out the hard way that "friend" doesn't always have the same meaning two days in a row.

Annie didn't eat lunch with me but came up to me at noon recess. "Fran, come over and we'll talk with Marcy and Sue. Let's get this thing straightened out so we can all be friends."

"I'm not going over there, Annie. Thanks anyway, but maybe you shouldn't get involved." I had a bad feeling about this, and I was irritated with Annie for butting into my business.

"Oh, Fran, how do you ever expect to make them your friends?" Annie almost shouted at me. But she lowered her voice at the last minute and waved the group over to us. "Come on; let's talk it over."

As they came over, Annie became all sweet and smiles. "Marcy, don't you like Fran?"

"What's there to like?" Marcy had a way of curling her lip that she thought made her look cool. To me she looked dumb, like Old Man Wessenfeld's Lab. "Fran always looks like she's just walked out of a hurricane. Or maybe she thinks that's the latest in hairdos." Marcy laughed as I imagined a hyena laughs.

Annie turned around then and asked me, quite seriously, "Yeah, Fran, why don't you do something about your hair?"

At this point, Annie was no longer my friend. Sue eyed me like I'd seen salespeople who want you to buy something from them. "And why don't you wear a bra, Fran? It's disgusting."

"Yeah!" agreed Marcy, enlightenment all over her face.

"Because I choose not to. Because I don't let anyone think for me, thanks anyway you guys."

Ursala walked away, and I liked her for that, although she was still Marcy's friend. I also left, knowing full well they stood there discussing my attributes. Maybe they should've tried to solve some of their own personality problems instead of mine.

During math, Annie slipped me a note, apologizing if my feelings had gotten hurt over what Marcy and the others had said at recess. Mrs. Hammershaw must have seen me take the note because next thing I know she was beside my desk, demanding I hand it over.

She called me to her desk for a conference. "What is this all about, Fran?"

"It's nothing, Mrs. Hammershaw. We had a discussion on the playground at noon is all."

So, of course, she called over Annie, Marcy, Sue, and Ursala to tell their versions. Marcy spoke up first.

"Fran wanted to know what we thought about her, so we told her that she could do something about the way her hair sticks up all over." Marcy wiggled all her fingers in the air over her head.

Mrs. Hammershaw eyed me. "Fran, in the future you might think twice about inviting criticism." She tapped the note with her finger. "And do you think, Marcy, that it is your moral duty to tell Fran what you think are her shortcomings?"

She blushed at that, and to tell you the truth, it made me feel good to see her uncomfortable while Mrs. Hammershaw stared at her. People always gave Marcy only compliments—"good going," "nice try," or "terrific idea!"—even when she'd goof up, and maybe she got a taste of how she could make others feel sometimes.

Mrs. Hammershaw looked down the line from Marcy to Sue to Ursala to Annie and, at last, to me. "I think you girls should give some thought to how your words can affect others. I'd like each of you, except for Fran, to write me a one-page paper on how the Golden Rule applies on the playground as well as in the classroom."

"Mrs.....Mrs. Hammershaw," I sort of stuttered. "We were just talking it over, like I said." I sure hated to see Ursala get into trouble over this since she hadn't really been in on any of it. It would have been so much better for me if no one had gotten into any trouble.

"Well, Fran, I'm sorry that this had to happen at all. I'm much too interested in what everyone has to say about their actions to let it go unnoticed." Mrs. Hammershaw folded the note in half and stuck in the top drawer of her desk. "You girls may go back to your seats."

Then she stood, as if she needed to watch each one of us to make sure we took our right seats. "Now, class, take out your math books and please start on page forty-one, set nine. I want this classroom quiet while I am in the office copying your English worksheet." When she left the room, I glanced around at the others.

If looks could have killed, I'd have been dead as lead. At that moment, I wondered if God disliked me, too. He must have had bigger worries than mine to take up His time because He sure wasn't helping me out.

I didn't say anything to my mom. I didn't want to hear any more advice from anyone, let alone from my mother. I just wanted at least a good showing at the volleyball games and to make it until the end of June without anymore confrontations. My grades were decent, and I would get another merit award for attendance at the school year's last assembly.

Or I would have, if the bully dogs hadn't cornered me the next day for what seemed like hours. There I stood, huddled against the knurly oak tree, waiting for one or all three beasts to attack me when the golden retriever whirled around, sniffed the air, and all of them took off after a cat. Because of them, I was late to school for the first time ever. I always got a merit award for zero tardies and absences, and now that little record was ruined.

At recess, I said practically nothing to Annie but hi and absolutely nothing to Marcy or Sue. Ursala and I exchanged a "Hi, how are you?" and even worked on a science project as partners. I felt kind of misplaced, but it didn't get any worse than that.

All the girls on the team showed up for game at Holy Rosary on Saturday. Marcy, Sue, Ursala, and

Annie went about their business as if I didn't exist, and we didn't have anything much to say to one another on the volleyball court. It made the game interesting, and I was very glad when it was over but sorry as anyone that we had lost it. We weren't out of the play-offs, but our chances of winning three games in a row were slim. Miss Ford told us we had played a good game against a tough team, but I wondered if we could have played better if we hadn't been mad at each other.

Sue and Marcy walked close by me, and Sue talked to Marcy loud enough to make sure I heard. "Next year, we'll have someone else other than Fran's mom get the coach's present, someone with better ideas."

I guess I could have told them that it would have been fine with my mom, I'm sure, but I didn't. If Marcy and the others really felt that way, why didn't they say it to my mom's face? It might have solved a lot of headaches for everyone, although I doubted Sue or Marcy could have gone up to my mom and said that to her. I didn't think they were that gutsy—or stupid.

On my way home from school Friday, I could see Old Man Wessenfeld's yard from across the street, and all three bully dogs were sitting in a row at the chain link fence, panting and looking like little kids pooped out from playing hard. The big black Lab cocked his head and watched me, while the cocker spaniel and bird dog tilted their heads so close together they almost touched noggins. They should have been circus dogs, or court jesters. And I would have been king for a day and commanded them and some other subjects. There'd be an end to some squabbling in my realm, for sure.

I just wished it were that easy. You know, easy like all the grown-ups say kids have got it. Things never are that easy, especially of course, if you're talking to an adult. Then your whole life gets complicated.

Chapter 8

Where's a Good Magician When You Need One?

"Well, Frances, how did your day go?" Mom asked as I came into the kitchen. She'd baked chocolate chip cookies, and the two biggest ones were still warm, perfect with cold milk.

I shrugged. "Nothing much to tell."

"Nothing, Frances? Are you sure?" She had that look that told me she knew something, but I couldn't figure out what.

"Huh?" I looked real hard at her, hoping to find a clue in her face.

"Mrs. Hammershaw called me today. About that incident on the playground."

"Oh, that. There's nothing really to tell, Mom. Annie, Marcy, Sue, Ursala, and I were talking, and really, that's between us, anyway."

"That's what I figured. I told Mrs. Hammershaw I thought the best thing to do was let you girls work it out."

Good, I thought, we wouldn't have to go into it anymore.

"But," she added with a dramatic pause, "you might give some thought to how much alike you and Marcy are."

I choked, not having expected anything like that from her. "No, way!" I sputtered.

She stood with her hands on her hips, her eyes piercing into my head to see how my brain worked. I tried not to move a muscle, just watching her as she continued.

"It takes two for a conflict. Without you, Marcy will find someone else to put down so she looks good. You're convenient because you're a volunteer."

She paused, I assumed, to let that sink into the many holes she'd just bored into my head. In a softer voice she added, "You'll have to face her, or someone like her, the rest of your life. You can't just wish your problems away, dear, because they come back at you like rabid dogs."

"Bully dogs," I groaned, feeling that Marcy and the bully dogs were a huge lump of concrete I had to carry in my backpack everyday.

"What bully dogs?" my mom asked, leaning across the counter on her elbows.

It had just slipped out, and I couldn't figure any-way to take it back. "Old Man...um...I mean, Mr. Wessenfeld's dogs. Sometimes they chase me on the way to school."

"And what do you do?" Leave it to my mom to ask the obvious.

"I run from them." I wished I could have just nipped another cookie from the plate without her seeing me.

Then she pointed to the plate. "Have one more and tell me how long has this been going on." She pushed those wonderful, chocolaty cookies toward me.

"They're usually out at seven-thirty. Most times they chase me to the school yard."

"Do they go after anyone else?" My mom looked at me, and suddenly those cookies lost their taste.

"No—um—I don't know! Sometimes they go after a cat or squirrel, or Mr. Wessenfeld calls them back."

"Frances," I could see that my mom was thinking, and that always spelled trouble for me, "I want you to go talk with Mr. Wessenfeld. Tell him you're having a problem with his dogs."

"Mom! I can't do that! No way am I going near those bloodthirsty dogs!!!!" I realized I had just shouted at my mom, and she was not looking real happy. "Mom," I begged. Sometimes it works, some-times it doesn't. "Can't you understand I can't go there? What am I supposed to do, walk through the yard right up to the front door? Those dogs wouldn't let me past the gate." My mom wasn't softening up one bit. "I don't know what to say to Mr. Wessenfeld. Can't you call him and explain things, please? You're an adult. You know, do it adult-to-adult."

She shook her ugly head no, and I thought I was going to be sick to my stomach. "I'm not going to do it." The tears came, but I didn't care. I imagined only too well what those bully dogs would do to me. "I'm too young to die like that."

She brushed the tears from my cheeks. "You're too young to let fear dominate you, Fran. Knowing how to be brave isn't reciting a spell or saying the right words like in the fairy tales; and you'll never find a book that gives you a simple, magic formula. The magic is inside yourself, here," she said, patting the place where my heart was about to go into cardiac arrest, "and here," as she touched my forehead. "You have to think yourself brave and then make yourself act bravely. Even though you're scared, you do what has to be done. Then, each time you tackle something you fear and overcome it, you've won a major battle for yourself. But you have to make up your mind to do it."

Sounded to me like I was off the hook. I dried my tears and nibbled on the rest of my cookie. "I'll go see Mr. Wessenfeld tomorrow."

My mom handed me a tissue. "No, you'll go see him today."

I didn't argue with her, not when she was standing in front of me looking like General Patton ordering his troops into battle. Only I wasn't sure if I could make myself go, that's how frightened I was.

"Then I might as well go right now." I don't know why I said that, maybe because I felt doomed anyway. "I'll change my clothes before I go."

"Oh, don't bother, honey. You can do that when you come home." My mom walked me down the hall, giving me a hug as she pushed me out the door.

I couldn't make myself move off the porch. In my head, I saw the bully dogs tearing into me as I walked into their yard. Well, at least my mom wouldn't get any money back at the school clothing exchange if she'd try to turn in my uniform all torn and bloodied.

I wondered if Carol and Pattie would come see me in the hospital. Maybe they'd bring me some games, like Hangman and Connect-Four. And books. I could read a lot if I were lying in bed all day waiting for my thousands of wounds to heal.

I couldn't stand there all day on the porch. The Wessenfeld's house seemed a lot closer than it usually did when I'd leave for school. By the time I got as far as the Patterson's house next door to the Wessenfeld's, the dogs were barking and jumping at the gate. I stayed right where I was on the sidewalk, like

I was frozen or something. Sweat trickled down my sides. I've heard dogs smell fear, and I'm sure I reeked enough that a dog clear over on the other side of town knew how scared I was. That probably made those bozos feel like the Super Dogs.

I couldn't believe my feet were moving! But I began inching along until I stepped onto the driveway and then stopped. I couldn't go on, and I couldn't go home. I stared at the dogs, and that made them crazier. I took little steps closer, and the black Lab charged the gate, making the posts creak. I stopped dead still. The dogs and I locked eyes, only they continued to bark, and I no longer had a voice to call for help or anything.

"Whaddya want?" Mr. Wessenfeld materialized out of nowhere, looming over the gate, waving a book at me. "If you're selling cookies, I don't want any. Go 'way."

I'm sure no one would want to sell him any cookies. Besides, it was almost May; the Girl Scout Cookie Drive was in February. And he couldn't make me disappear with a wave and command, not when I'd gotten this close. "No!" popped out of my mouth, and real loud, too!

Mr. Wessenfeld looked at me as if I had three heads and green hair. "Whaddya mean, 'no'?"

I shook my head, more to loosen my thoughts than anything else. "I'm not selling cookies. I came over to talk to you." I pointed. "About them. They chase me every morning when you let them out."

"Aw, they won't hurt you. Stop running from them." He started to turn and go back inside his house.

"No, Mr. Wessenfeld!" I had to make him understand that it hadn't been that easy for me with his dogs. The dogs whined, and the Lab eyed me, probably sizing me up for his dinner. "I don't like them chasing me all the way to school. You've got to make them stop it!"

"I do, do I? And just what makes you think that?" He folded his arms across his chest as he leaned against the gate post, staring me down. I wished I had the power to turn him into a rock.

We stared at each other for a long time, and my head began to pound, and I squinted at him even harder. He had dared me to answer him, and I was going to. Only right then, I forgot what I was going to say.

Chapter 9

A New Perspective

I felt like someone's hands were around my throat, strangling me so I couldn't tell Old Man Wessenfeld that I thought his dogs should be kept in the yard and not be allowed out to chase me every day to school. He still stood at the gate, and I still stood on his driveway, and we still stared at each other. I don't know what would have happened if Mrs. Wessenfeld hadn't come out just then.

"Why, isn't it Frances Reed, Mary's daughter? My, it's been such a long time since I've seen you!" She stood on the bottom step of their porch, drying her hands on a dish towel.

"Hi, Mrs. Wessenfeld." I felt somewhat embarrassed, like I should have explained why I hadn't been around in a while, that I hadn't joined the Girl Scouts this year, so I didn't have to sell any cookies. Instead,

I shifted from foot to foot, watching the dogs dance around her, whining like dogs do for attention.

"George, open the gate for Frances so that she can come inside. I've just made some fresh lemonade and have an extra cold glass on hand. Come along and let's chat for a spell."

I was terrified when Mr. Wessenfeld unlatched the gate and it swung open. The dogs, yipping and scuffling, made a dash for me. I braced myself, expecting to be eaten alive.

The Lab plowed into my legs, just about knocking me to the ground. The cocker spaniel sniffed my shoes, while the golden retriever nudged my hand, as if to make me pet him.

"You see, young lady," Mr. Wessenfeld adjusted his thick, black-framed glasses, while pointing to each dog, "Aramis, Porthos, and Athos won't hurt you."

I looked right at Mr. Wessenfeld. He might have thought highly of his precious pets, but I certainly didn't. And I didn't think much of their names coming from such noble characters. "The Three Musketeers? You can't be serious!"

"My goodness, no!" chirped Mrs. Wessenfeld, flipping the dish towel over her shoulder. "I really think they're more like the Three Stooges!"

That certainly fit the image I had of them lined up at the fence, looking kind of goofy. I started giggling, which made them even more playful around me, so much so that I couldn't move without pushing them out of the way as I walked. Finally, I just stopped and petted each one, keeping my face away from the flapping tongue of the big, black Lab, Aramis, as he tried to lick me. Porthos, the cocker spaniel, brought over a ball, which I threw, and all three dashed for it, leaving me just enough time to scoot by Mr. Wessenfeld and through the front door where I met Mrs. Wessenfeld. She handed me a glass of iced lemonade.

I almost sucked it all down, but I remembered how annoyed my mom got with me when I did that, so I took about four gulps to finish it. I gave Mrs. Wessenfeld back the glass. "Thank you."

"Come into the kitchen and I'll pour you and George another glass."

Mr. Wessenfeld followed me as I followed Mrs. Wessenfeld. I was reminded of a scene from *Heidi*, probably because of the happy feeling I got when I walked into the sunny kitchen with big windows lined in planters of blooming marigolds, pansies, and impatiens and home-baked bread right out of the oven.

"Wednesday's baking day for me. I'll send you home with a loaf." Mrs. Wessenfeld dusted off a loaf of white bread, sprinkling crumbs along the counter, and then turned around. She sort of chuckled, her hands on her hips, her face soft with a big smile. "I can't get out of the habit of making enough to feed a family of six, although it's just George and I nowadays." She tilted her head, her eyes twinkling. "If you don't count the dogs, that is. And they're just like children in a lot of ways, but we don't let them eat at our table."

I thought she was funny and warm and kind. She looked a whole lot different than my granny, taller and plumper, but she felt like the kind of grandmother every kid would like to have. I didn't know much about grandfathers, but I just couldn't imagine why she had married such an old grouch like George. However, I didn't say anything about that. "I came over to ask if you'd keep the Three Musketeers in the yard on school mornings. They chase me, sometimes all the way to Saint Mary's."

Mr. Wessenfeld sat down in a bar stool at the far end of the kitchen counter, laying his book cover up so that I sneaked a peek at the title, *Mything Persons*. It took me totally by surprise that he, of all people, would be interested in a science fantasy book, especially a series that dealt with magicians, dragons, and demons and had puns for chapter headings. For a moment, I forgot that I didn't like Mr. Wessenfeld.

"Did you know that *Mything* books are a whole series?" I sort of blurted it out, catching Mr. Wessenfeld off guard. He jerked upright in his seat, picked up the book, looked at the cover, then me.

"Didn't give it much thought. My grandson gave me some books to read when I was in the hospital, and I'm just getting around to this one."

"You should read them in sequence, you know. It makes more sense that way, and you can keep track of all the new characters and past events," I pointed out logically enough.

He looked at me like I had spoken about an R-rated movie that a kid shouldn't know anything about. "So you say."

I thought it too bad Mrs. Wessenfeld had to live with such a grump. She crunched foil around the loaf of bread and set it in front of me where I stood by the end of the counter. "Now, don't forget to take this home, Fran. You must read a lot; you seem to know so much about books." Her voice had a nice lilt to it as she spoke.

"Oh, yeah, I do." I nodded, working an end of pinched foil back and forth. "Eight, nine books in a week. Sometimes more, especially in the summer, if my mom doesn't have chores for me to do."

"Goodness! You and George! You two should have a lot to talk about! He reads all the time, more now that he's recuperating from his stroke. Pretty soon, though, he'll be back to his routine and exercising the dogs regularly." She stopped and tapped her finger alongside of her face. "Oh, that's right, you've come to talk about a problem with our intrepid trio."

Mr. Wessenfeld interrupted her. "I don't see she has one. The dogs won't bother her now that they know her." He almost smiled at me, I thought.

I hadn't thought of that. It seemed I didn't have a problem, anymore. I also didn't have anything else to say.

Mrs. Wessenfeld steepled her fingers, pressing them against her lips, as if she was lost for a moment in her thoughts, before she spoke. "Fran, I just thought of something." She paused and looked at me.

I knew that adult-look, and it gave me the shivers. I was being sized up by Mrs. Wessenfeld, but I was curious to know what her scheme was all about.

"Do you think your parents would let you have a part-time job after school?" She arched an eyebrow, knowing full well she'd snagged my attention. "If you would like a job, how about exercising the dogs on leashes?"

"You know," Mr. Wessenfeld cleared his throat, "it'd be like you were the caboose behind the steam engine."

I liked that, the way he put it. I'd probably still huff and puff, but at least I'd get paid for it, and I'd be running behind the bully dogs instead of in front of them. Although, now, it was kind of hard to think of the Three Musketeers as mean. Really, they were only silly dogs that needed to let off some energy.

"I'm sure my mom wouldn't mind if I did it after school. Except for Tuesdays, and I could do it later, after my piano lesson."

Mr. Wessenfeld made a sour face, which made him look sort of like a dried-out apple. "Why is it all children take piano lessons? It's not the only instrument worth playing."

Mrs. Wessenfeld clucked her tongue. "Don't mind George. He's played the trumpet since he was nine but couldn't get one of our four kids interested. But he still plays in a quartet at least once a month at the Elks."

I mean, could you believe this? I sort of laughed and shook my head. "I play the trumpet, too. Miss Kray says I'll make first chair before school's out, the first time a girl's done that!" I know it sounded like bragging, but it was the truth.

"Well," groused Mr. Wessenfeld, "you have more sense than any of my own children or grandchildren. But I like you anyway." He waited to see if I'd laugh, which I didn't. But I smiled.

"You have any of Asprin's other books?" he asked, rather nicely for him, I thought.

"Yeah!" I nodded, so hard I almost gave myself whiplash. "I've got the whole series."

He stood up, book in hand, and started walking towards what looked like his den. "Tell you what,

Franny old girl. Bring me the first two, and maybe we can trade some books from library. Deal?"

"Deal, Mr. Wessenfeld." I scooped up the still-warm loaf of bread, matching smiles with Mrs. Wessenfeld. "Thanks. I'll ask my mom about walking the dogs and let you know."

She walked me to the door, where three wet noses instantly appeared in the opening. "Or just come by after school tomorrow," she suggested.

When I stepped outside, I immediately became tangled up in wanna-be playmates. I kept the bread high over my head as I made my way to the gate, stopping to scratch first Athos behind the ear, then Porthos, and giving an extra minute to Aramis because he laid his big, black head in my hand with a huge, contented sigh before he let me go on my way.

Chapter 10

Winning Combinations

I hugged the warm loaf of bread, liking the crunching sound of the foil as well as the aroma as I pressed my nose and inhaled as much as I could. Up the far end of the street I could see Dean delivering the evening paper. He looked my way and saw me, then waved back. "Hey, Fran!" he yelled, and I skipped down the street to meet him.

"Hi, Dean." I fell in step with him. He pitched a newspaper right smack in the middle of the Simmons' front stoop. "Hey, that's pretty good!"

Dean smiled and shrugged. "That's because I practice pitching a lot. My dad spends every Saturday coaching me. Like every weekend we play catch or one-on-one."

"Well, you're lucky. I only get a lot of advice, mostly from my mom." He looked at me as if I had meant it to be funny so I smiled pretending I had.

"No, Fran, you're luck-lucky." I'd almost forgotten he stuttered until then.

"Why am I lucky? You're not the one who has to listen to my mom lecturing me all the time."

"Because." He stopped, folded a paper and shoved it into a newspaper box. "It's just my-my dad and me."

I suddenly felt kind of sad, for I'd heard rumors Dean lived alone with his dad, but I hadn't thought much about it. "Gosh, that must be tough, not having a mother."

Dean squinted as he looked at me, and I could see in his eyes that it hurt him to talk about this. I wished I could have somehow shared my mom with him, which made me want to wrap my arms around her and give her the biggest hug ever.

I thought it best to change the subject altogether. "You know, you're awfully good at basketball. I watched part of the game the other day."

"I'm all right. I know I'll never be a st-star, but I'm good enough to play on the team."

"I wish I were as good." I didn't mean to sound all sorry for myself because I had been feeling pretty good about the way things had gone, after all, today.

"That's just it—you-you are, Fran. S-s-some of the other guys think so, too. You just let Marcy bully you.

You don't have to take that, you know. She might be athletic, and Ursala, too, but two people don't make a team. I don't want to be like Steve or Chase. It's okay by me if they want to be superstars. I don't mind being just a team player."

"It doesn't seem fair that others can't just leave you alone." I was thinking about him and me, too. "You know, let you do your best and leave it at that."

"That's what I was trying to say. You just got to do it. If you can't ignore Marcy; stand up to her."

I looked at him, not really mad or anything. "Everyone's got advice to give, huh?"

He laughed. "Yeah. Like my dad says, 'Take mine; it's free.'"

"Do you deliver papers the same time every day?" We were getting close to my house, and I wanted to share my good news. "I'll probably see you almost everyday."

"Just about. It's a pretty large paper route. You thinking about getting a route of your own?"

"No, I got a job walking the Wessenfelds' dogs." I pointed at their house, and the Three Musketeers were lined up at the fence, watching us, as if they were at the movies and we were actors on the screen.

"Boy! That'll be a sight to see! I can't wait!" Dean slapped a newspaper into the next box. "Fran s-s-streaking down the street."

That was kind of funny, but I wanted him to know I could handle the dogs. "They're not that bad. Mr. Wessenfeld said they're really good on leashes. How far does your route go?"

"Over to Main and Camellia."

"Yes, I guess I will see you when I'm out with the dogs."

"Yeah, that'd be all right." We came to my house, and Dean handed me a newspaper, sort of hanging onto to it for a minute until he had finished speaking. "Maybe you could come over to my house on the weekend, and we could shoot some baskets. I'll show you some things I know that might help you."

"Thanks." I waved good-bye, wrapping the newspaper around the loaf of bread and went in the back door to the living room.

I sat awhile in my dad's chair, wondering if I couldn't make things better for myself at school, too, with Marcy and Sue, and maybe patch up the holes in the friendship with Annie. How much worse could it be than what I'd gone through today? I was probably as scared as I ever remember being in my whole life, yet I managed to get through it. I mean, I went into enemy territory and came out with a loaf of bread, a job, and some mighty unexpected friends, like the Wessenfelds and the Three Musketeers. Even better, I had a new source of paperback books that the local branch library seems to be so short of every week. Dean made it sound easy enough to stand up for myself, and I felt that I could make myself do anything I had a mind to do.

Well, it looked as if the only way I could find out if there was anything to this magic streak of mine was to give Marcy a call. I put the bread on my lap, sniffing that wonderful aroma as I dialed Marcy's number from the downstairs telephone. "Uh, Marcy? This is Fran."

I expected her to slam the phone down in my ear, but she didn't, just breathed real hard and waited for me to continue. "I didn't think it was right that Mrs. Hammershaw made you guys write that essay."

"You can spare me your sympathy, Franny. I don't want it."

"You know Marcy," I shot back, "you didn't have any real good reasons for not liking me. If that's really important."

I figured I had her attention and could keep her listening for another minute. "You don't have to like me, but I think it hurts our team when we can't get along. I think we lost that last game because we couldn't concentrate on the plays, like Miss Ford said. And we both know we can't afford to lose anymore games."

"So you're not going to come to anymore games, Fran?" It sounded like Marcy started out wanting to be sarcastic, and then changed her mind. "Of course, I didn't mean that." But then she added, "I wouldn't want you to tell anyone I said that."

This was getting me nowhere, faster than I wanted to go. "You think you can win the game by yourself, Marcy? You're good, but not that good, and most of the other girls think so, too. At least six people told me they wished you would stop trying so hard to do it all yourself. The idea is to be the best team, not the best player."

"I don't believe that six people would even talk to you, Franny Fruitcake!" she snarled, about to hang up, I'm sure.

"Wait, Marcy! You know it's true! Only Ursala, Annie, and Sue talked to you after our last game. And half the team told Miss Ford that they didn't really care if we made the play-offs or not. Just ask Miss Ford." I listened to Marcy's angry breathing even out then felt it safe to go on.

"Look, Marcy, we have two more practices before the next big game. I don't want to be your best friend or anything, but I don't like us being mean to one another, either. I'm going to be there, and I'm going to sign up for basketball, too." The funny thing was I hadn't felt all that brave until I said aloud what I meant to do. I guess I might have come right out and said, "Let's make a deal," but I couldn't quite do that.

She heaved a sigh, and I thought I was in for a rash of irritation. "We're stuck with one another, then, huh, Fran?"

I waited for the nasty aside that didn't come, so I spoke up. "Yeah, we're stuck with one another."

"We get on each other's nerves, you know?" She was tapping on something, and the little ticking sounds echoed in the receiver.

"Yeah, like a bad habit." I thought about what I had said and hurried to add, "But, hey, we could break a bad habit, you know?"

"Yeah, maybe. I've got to go, Fran."

"See you tonight at practice, Marcy." She hadn't hung up mad, at least she hadn't sounded as if she was mad, and I thought maybe she would think it over.

I felt pretty certain that Marcy and I were going to find a way to get along. But just what would I do if things continued on the same way? I drummed my fingers on the table, thinking.

Well, for one thing, I concluded, I wasn't the same, so what would happen wouldn't be the same either. I had made my mind up about playing on the volleyball and basketball team, doing my best, and being a good team player, and right now, I felt really good about myself.

I slipped the newspaper on the seat of my dad's easy chair as I made my way into the kitchen where my mom was fixing dinner. I dropped the bread on the kitchen counter by the sink, then gave Mom a big bear hug and smacked a kiss on her cheek.

"Whatever was that for?" she asked, obviously surprised.

"Oh, because." I scraped carrot peelings into the garbage and searched through the drawer for a black tie to twist around the top of the liner, making tracks for the back door. She just smiled when I told her about my job walking the dogs and how Mr. Wessenfeld wanted to trade books with me.

She looked real pleased when she spied the loaf of bread. "Did you remember...?"

"Yes, I remembered to say 'thank you.'" I slid the shiny, foiled loaf along counter, then gave it a shove into her cupped hands. "And I know I still have to change my clothes, practice the piano and the trumpet, and do my homework. Are we having anything good for dinner?"

"Since you're feeling so sassy, how about clam chowder?"

I grabbed my throat and pretended to choke to death because she knew I hated clam chowder even more than spinach. "If I don't do all those things, what'll we have?" That made her laugh, and I knew I'd scored a "gotcha."

"We're having your favorite tonight, Frances, steak and potatoes." I gave a loud whoop for joy, but then she added, "And broccoli."

Well, I guess you can't have everything 100-percent perfect. "Peaches for dessert?" I asked hopefully.

She nodded, pointing to Mrs. Wessenfeld's loaf of bread. "It'll still be warm and delicious, too."

"Yeah. You know what, Mom?" I snitched a cookie, knowing she'd let it go this time. "I called Marcy, and I think we've made a deal to get along. I bet you see a big difference at our next game."

Mom looked sort of surprised; more like stunned. I smiled at her as I swiped the last cookie on the plate and headed for my room. I had in mind that I'd go over to Dean's house late Sunday afternoon and shoot some baskets, then leash up the Three Musketeers to get them used to me walking them. That way, it wouldn't be too hard to get into a new routine on Monday.

I had just about completed the last question at the end of the chapter review of "Water and Our Environment" when Annie called. "Hi, Fran. I didn't copy down the science assignment. Did you?"

I had a funny feeling that she hadn't really forgotten to do it at all. Her mom never let her use the telephone until after all her homework was done. "Yeah, it's chapter eleven review questions on page fifty-eight."

"Oh, great, that's what I thought." There was this pause long enough for a television commercial. "Uh, Fran, I really am sorry about what happened. I don't want you to be mad about it."

Mad? Who me? I wanted to say but didn't. "Aw, it's all right, I guess."

"You're going to practice tonight, aren't you?"

"Yeah, are you?" I know she is, because she never misses a practice session or a game.

"My mom can take me, but I need a ride home. Do you think your mom can bring me home?"

Boy, did I want to say something, like why didn't she ask Marcy or Sue for a ride home, but suddenly I thought maybe Annie was trying to be my friend again. Why not? She had to write that stupid paper, and I could see that things were pretty even now between us.

"Hang on a minute and I'll ask." I knew my mom would say yes, which she does. "It's okay, Annie."

"Great! Well, I guess I better go. We'll really have to work on our serves tonight, won't we?"

"Yeah, but I think our team can get it together. We're all really pretty good, as a team."

"Yeah, Fran, you can say that again. Well, 'bye."

I didn't have to say it again, because Miss Ford told us after practice that we looked terrific and she thought we could make the play-offs with no sweat.

I don't know about the "no sweat" part, but we turned out to be a winning a team, after all. Marcy came over to me after the game, as everyone was leaving, and made it a point to shake hands with me, adding in an undertone, "Good game, Fran. We're the best girls' team around." I couldn't have agreed more.

Annie and I got back to being friends, but we saw each other mostly at school, not so much on the weekends, anymore. Which was all right, because I got so busy with my new job walking the Three Musketeers and shooting baskets Sunday afternoon with Dean and his dad that I didn't have a whole lot of time for doing the things Annie liked to do with Marcy, Sue, and Ursala. Pattie and Carol came over sometimes, and then all of us would go over to the schoolyard or Dean's house.

Fourteen girls tried out for seventh-grade girls' basketball, which made our coach, Miss Ford, very happy. Maybe—no, more than maybe—we had another winning team.